Nobody Sleeps

by Guernsey Le Pelley

Baker's Plays
7611 Sunset Blvd.
Los Angeles, CA 90042
bakersplays.com

NOBODY SLEEPS

CHARACTERS

Spike, *a burglar, and not a very good one, about* 40
Daisy Busby, *16*
Ada Busby, *18* } *sisters*
Glory Busby, *20*
Mrs. Busby, *mother of the girls; a would-be novelist*

SYNOPSIS

The scene is the library in the Busby home Midnight of the present year. The season and the exact location of the Busby home are immaterial.

PREMIERE PERFORMANCE

Noboby Sleeps was first presented at the Gila Junior College Little Theatre, Thatcher, Arizona, under the direction of W Clayton Kauffman, with the following cast:

SPIKE ....*Burl Booth*

DAISY BUSBY .... *Dorothy Gardner*

ADA BUSBY ....*Mavis Moffett*

GLORY BUSBY ....*Roxy Hawkins*

MRS. BUSBY ... .*Sybil Nelson*

PRODUCTION NOTES

*T*HERE is little need for production notes in a play like *Nobody Sleeps*. There is nothing about the set that cannot be changed to meet the exigencies of the moment. The position of doors and the French windows is suggested, but if it seems easier to rearrange the stage to meet conditions, it should be a simple matter to do so. A small sofa, a desk, and one chair will suffice for furniture if space is at a premium. Curtains will do quite as well as a set made of flats. The costume problem is nil; the lighting, simplicity itself. Such a play lends itself to production almost anywhere, and it should find favor as a contest play, both because of its intrinsic humor and for the ease with which it may be played under strange conditions away from home, on a stage that supplies (as in most state contests) only the barest necessities.

As for hand properties, Spike has a flashlight and a gun; Daisy, a tray of sandwiches. Add to these a litter of books and papers on the desk, and a desk telephone, and the job is complete. Somebody's going to pen a note of thanksgiving for a play that is drolly funny and interesting to the last line . . . one practically cancelling the manual labor attendant upon play production, and giving the cast and director a chance to centralize on acting.

NOBODY SLEEPS

One cannot immediately see the charm of the Busby library, because it happens to be in the middle of the night. The lights are out, and the Busbys are asleep . . . or should be. However, there is moonlight which we can see lighting a balcony through the French doors U.C.

U L. is a desk, littered with papers and books. A regulation desk chair is near at hand. D.L. is a large, comfortable chair, and at R. is a sofa, another comfortable chair, and a coffee table. Other furnishings as desired.

U.L. an arch leads to a stairway and to a hall that leads to the front door. At R. is a swinging door to the kitchen.

Soon a figure appears outside the French doors U.C., and climbs up on the balcony. It is SPIKE, *a burglar. He examines the doors. After a little manipulation, he opens the doors and comes into the room, closing the doors quietly behind him. He surveys the room professionally with a flashlight, then goes to the arch U.L., listens attentively, crosses to the door R., opens it a trifle, listens, then comes back to room C. After a moment's thought, he goes to the desk and begins to search through the drawers. Suddenly he becomes alert, for he thinks he hears something. He does hear something. Someone is whistling softly, "Here We Go 'Round the Mulberry Bush." Though it is very faint at first, it grows louder as the whistler comes down the stairs.*

It turns out to be DAISY, very young, very pretty, and attired in a dressing gown.

SPIKE snaps out the flashlight just before DAISY enters the room, still whistling. She snaps on the light from a switch near the arch U.L., and crosses R. toward the kitchen door.

Spike. (*As DAISY reaches the kitchen door, pointing a gun at her.*) Stop right where you are!

(*DAISY stops obediently without turning, but doesn't stop whistling.*)

Put up your hands!

(*She does so . . . still whistling.*)

And stop whistling, you dope!

Daisy. (*Trying to get a look.*) Are you a burglar?

Spike. What do you think I am? Your fairy Godmother? Turn around!

Daisy. (*Turning to him.*) Gee, that's swell, if you're a real burglar Stick around. Mother'll want to see you. She writes mystery stories.

(*DAISY crosses to C.*)

Spike. That's too bad Keep your hands up.

Daisy. Now, what's the sense in keeping my hands up? In detective stories the only reason they make people put their hands up is so they can't reach for a gun, and any half-witted, decrepit burglar could see I haven't got a gun in my dressing gown.

Spike. All right, put 'em down then, but no funny business. (*Pocketing the gun.*) I got work to do.

(*He goes back to the desk*)

Daisy. You'll never find anything in that desk We never can.

Spike. I'll get along Just pipe down.

Daisy.   I was just going to get a midnight snack . . . cold turkey sandwich   Can I make you one?

Spike.   No   If I get hungry, I'll make my own turkey sandwich!

Daisy.   Say . you're not a friend of Mother's, are you?

(SPIKE *turns and gives her full attention.*)

Spike.   Dames are sure dumb   If I was an old friend of your mother's, what would I be doing prowling around the house?

Daisy.   I don't know

Spike.   Well, then, stop asking dumb questions.

Daisy.   Do you know Father?

Spike.   Now, you listen here

Daisy.   That isn't a dumb question   We have some awfully funny friends   You could prowl around the house and still be a friend of the family's   sort of a week-end guest

Spike.   Let's get it straight   I don't even know your family. I'm not a friend of yours!   I prowl around the house, and I'm not a friend of yours

(SPIKE *crosses* D C.)

Daisy.   All right, all right.

(*After a pause in which* SPIKE *looks about uneasily, wondering what to do next*)
Do you know Ada?

Spike.   (*With a sigh*)   Who's Ada?

Daisy.   My sister. Then I have a sister named Glory, too.

Spike.   I don't know any of 'em   What's more, I don't want to know any of 'em.

Daisy.   My name's Daisy

Spike.   I don't care   I don't want to know you either!

Daisy.   I'll tell you where my sister keeps her money, if you'll cut me in on it.

8

Spike.   Where?

Daisy.   What's my split?

Spike.   All right, kid, if you want to play games, I'll give you ten per cent Where is it?

Daisy.   Oh, phooey   That'll only give me sixteen cents

Spike.   Sixteen cents!   You mean the money you're talking about is a dollar and sixty cents?

Daisy.   Well, how much did you expect to get out of this house? She's saving up for a guitar, so I'd just as soon you'd take the money Yeah, we all would

Spike.   Don't try to kid me   there's more money around here than a dollar and sixty cents My only problem *now* is what to do with *you*

Daisy.   Do you want to do something with me?

Spike.   I'd love to tap you with a pipe

Daisy.   Oh, I just came down to get a midnight snack   .
I won't bother   (*She suddenly decides*)   If you'll excuse me, I'll go out and get my sandwich now

> (*In a flash, she has turned and marched out through the kitchen door before* SPIKE *has a chance to realize what has happened*)

Spike.   Here! Wait a minute   . you!

> (*He starts across the room quickly, then moves more cautiously*)

Doggone that little dumb kid! It just shows you can never trust a dame

> (*He is just sneaking up to the kitchen door when* ADA *enters from the stairs, also in negligée. She is a year or so older than* DAISY. *Another chip off the old block.*)

Ada.   Is Daisy down here?

Spike.   (*Whirling around, gun in hand*)   Hands up!

Ada. (*Putting her hands up.*) Where's Daisy?

Spike. "Where's Daisy! Where's Daisy!" She *said* she was going to make a turkey sandwich

Ada. I might have known She eats enough to make any normal person fat, but I guess nobody can prove Daisy's normal
(*She crosses R.C.*)
Can I put my hands down? I'm beginning to feel awfully silly.

Spike. All right, put 'em down. (*Pocketing the gun.*) Things are silly enough around here already

Ada. (*With a little laugh.*) Oh you're cute. Are you a friend of Daisy's?

Spike. No I'm not.

Ada. I don't blame you. You'll like Glory and me better Stick around and I'll get Glory.
(*She turns to go U.L.*)

Spike. Wait a minute! Come back here! You ain't goin' to get anybody This place is crowded enough as it is.

Ada. Maybe you're right But Glory will be sore if we don't call her. Is Daisy making any coffee? Turkey sandwiches aren't much without coffee

Spike. Look! There's no sandwiches! No coffee! This ain't a picnic of the Campfire Girls I'm busy! All I want is to get finished with my work and get outa here. (*Suspiciously.*) Is there a telephone in that kitchen?
(*He crosses to the kitchen door and listens.*)

Ada. No. But there's one there on the desk. Put a dime in the box, if you call Laurelwood. That's a toll

Spike. I don't want to call up!

Ada. You just asked if we had a telephone.

Spike. I just want to know is that dame calling up.

Ada. Daisy? Who would she call up at this hour?

Spike. I suppose the *cops* never entered your fuzzy little head!

Ada. That's a cute idea. Sometime we ought to have a phone put in the kitchen in case of emergency.

Spike. All you people must be screwy.

(DAISY *enters R. with sandwich. She swings open the kitchen door . . . almost hitting* SPIKE, *and breezes into the room.*)

Daisy. Hello, Ada. Where'd he go?

Ada. He's still here.

(*She points.*)

Daisy. (*Turning*) Oh, there you are I was afraid you'd gone Have you met my sister Ada? Ada, this is . . . what was your name?

Spike. Never mind my name.

Daisy. (*To* ADA, *crossing L.*) He's kind of hard to get along with a first He's a burglar.

Ada. Oh, that's dandy! Why didn't you call Mother?

Spike. (*Coming to R.C.*) Listen, you!

Daisy. He doesn't want to meet Mother.

Ada. (*To* SPIKE.) You ought to meet Mom. You'd love her. She's been trying to get acquainted with a good burglar. Besides, she's trying to write a mystery story, you know.

Spike. (*Going U.C.*) Yeah, yeah, I know, I know.

Ada. (*To* DAISY) Why doesn't he want to meet her?

Daisy. I don't know, but he's kind of anti-social He wouldn't even eat a sandwich with me

Ada. Where did you get him?

Daisy. I didn't *get* him, stupid I found him here when I came down, standing there in the dark like a dope.

Ada. In here? How did he get in?

Daisy. I don't know. (*To* SPIKE.) How did you get in?

Spike. (*Indicating*) Through these doors (*Taking a menacing step toward them.*) Now, will you kindly shut up, before you wake up the whole neighborhood! If you don't pipe down right away, I'll have to tie you both to a chair and gag you

Ada. Oh, don't try to be melodramatic. You haven't anything to tie us up with

Daisy. He could hit us over the head with something

Ada. Never mind figuring things out for him.

Spike. I could do plenty And don't worry, I can figure things out for myself without a couple of dames puttin' their oar in But first of all, where do you keep all your dough?

Daisy. What dough?

Spike. You heard me You have t' keep some cash around here some place Where is it?

Daisy. I told him where your guitar money was, but he wouldn't take it

Ada. Where's the house money?

Daisy. In the pantry, I guess, unless Mom used it.

Ada. No, she's been here all day (*To* SPIKE.) It's in that silly china mug on the second shelf in the pantry It's sure bank night for you There must be over a dollar in it

Spike. Over a dollar! What kind of talk is that?

Daisy. You needn't turn up your nose. That, with Ada's guitar money, would be nearly three dollars

> (GLORY *enters from stairs. She is the eldest of the sisters, being twenty, but less dignified She is wearing a well-worn bathrobe.*)

Glory. Why didn't you tell me you were having a party?

Spike. Another one! (*Pointing the gun.*) Stick 'em up!
> (GLORY *puts her hands up as high as she can reach.*)

12

Ada. (*To* GLORY.) We were going to get you in a little while. Have you got any money?

Glory. Sure. There's a half a dollar on my dresser. How much do you need?

Daisy. (*To* SPIKE) What's your quota?

Spike. Now, listen, you! I'm not working for peanuts! (*To* GLORY.) And for Pete's sake put your hands down! I'm sorry I mentioned it!

(GLORY *puts her hands down*)

Glory. Thanks Would you like a turkey sandwich?

Spike. No I wouldn't

Glory. Well, *I'd* like a turkey sandwich. Why can't we all have some?

Daisy. Why not? I'll fix some up

(*In a whirl, she is gone out R.*)

Spike. Just a minute!

(*But he is too slow The door swings shut behind* DAISY)

Glory. (*Casually, as she crosses to the sofa*) Well   . who's your friend?

Ada. (*Sitting at L.*) I don't know He won't tell anybody his name

Glory. (*Turning*) Why? Where did he come from?

Ada. He's Daisy's Anyway Daisy said she found him here. He's a burglar

Glory. (*Mildly surprised. Sitting on sofa*) Oh . . . burglar   then

Spike. Yes, I know "Why don't you have him meet Mother? She's trying to write a mystery book "

Glory. Oh, then you know Are you a friend of Mother's?

Spike. No, I'm not! Can't any of you get that straight? I'm not a friend of nobody's I'm just here trying to do a quiet job of robbing a house without any interference!

Glory. Are you really a burglar, who came to rob the house?

Spike. Do I have to explain everything to everyone that comes along? I suppose sooner or later the whole town will come walking through this room.

Ada. It's a saying, you know! Sooner or later everyone in the world will pass through the Busby library

Spike. Oh, ye Gods!

Glory. Tell me, how did you get in?

Spike. Why do you insist on being so rude?

Glory. (*To* ADA.) I suppose he got through that door in the back hall . . I always said we ought to put a lock on it

Ada. No He didn't even know the back door was unlocked. (*Indicating.*) He busted through those doors

Glory. (*To* SPIKE.) Did you?

Spike. Yes, I did. Why?

Glory. But then you had to come across the front terrace.

Spike. So what?

Glory. So what? How can you call yourself a burglar, and walk across a newly seeded lawn? You've left at least a dozen footprints.

Spike. Aw . . . footprints! I don't believe in all that Sherlock Holmes stuff

Ada. Oh, you don't! You wouldn't *say* that if you'd read Mother's mystery book, "Sleeping People" In Mother's book they catch lots of crooks that way

Spike. Okay I'll remember that the next time I walk through one of her books.

Glory. Don't be a stupe! Anybody knows about footprints. From those footprints a detective can tell who you are, where you came from, the kind of walk you have, how tall you are, and how much you weigh

Spike.   And maybe where I stole the shoes   But don't worry   I usually get away all right

Glory.   That's another stupid remark   What good does it do to get away if you've left enough evidence to get caught in the next chapter

Ada.   He isn't even wearing gloves   I suppose he'll tell you his hands aren't cold

Spike.   Listen, all of you!   I don't wanna hear any more of this story-book stuff   I wasn't born yesterday

Ada.   I suppose not   Anyone born yesterday would know you're leaving a trail of fingerprints all over this house   You must have been born late this morning   Footprints and finger-prints   Ha!   Honest to Pete, you make it so easy for the cops you ought to be drawing a salary from the city

Spike.   Now, you listen to me

Glory.   (*Suddenly.*)   I'll bet you came here in a car and parked it in Chestnut Lane at the end of the street

Spike.   Sure I did.   How did you know?   Ain't Chestnut Lane a dark enough corner to hide a car in?

Ada   It's a nice dark corner, all right   It's too dark   It's the first place a cruising squad car always looks, just for love birds   I'll bet they take your license

Spike.   Well   I

Glory.   You'll probably find a cop waiting for you when you go back

Spike.   All right, Philo Vance, where would you have parked the car?

Glory   Why there's lots of good places for it.

Spike.   Yeah?

Glory. Yeah! You might have parked it down the street in front of Smith's They're having a party, and an extra car in front of the house wouldn't be noticed

Ada. Better still, you could have left your car at home and taken a bus

Glory. Why, your car would be even less conspicuous parked right in front of our house (*Thinking it over*) Yes . . . if I were robbing this house, I think I'd rather fancy parking my car right in front It has a sort of bravado to it

Ada. I think he's made a worse mistake than his car

Glory. His clothes!

Ada Yes!

Spike (*Dismally*) I don't have to take this from you. There's nothing the matter with my clothes I suppose you're going to say they're not the style for burglars

Ada. That's just it! They *are* the style for burglars!

Glory. Very much so If I were a cop passing you on the street, I'd say to myself, "There's a burglar if I ever saw one!"

Ada. Don't you see? It's obviously your job *not* to look like a burglar Why don't you wear a business suit and carry a brief case?

Spike. For one reason, I haven't got a brief case.

Ada. (*To* GLORY.) Haven't we got an old one of Dad's around? (*She turns to* SPIKE) Yes, I'm sure we have an old one upstairs we'll sell you

Glory. He wouldn't have to buy it He could steal it

Ada. I know, but that wouldn't be ethical, now that we've given him the tip and everything

Spike. Never mind going on like this. I'll get along all right . without a brief case!

Glory. (*Peevishly*) No one's so perfect he can't listen to suggestions.

Spike. What are you trying to do, scare me? What's the use of all this gabbing? (*An idea suddenly hits him.*) You couldn't by any chance be tryin' to stall me so that . . .

(*He goes toward the kitchen door, stops, calls.*)
Listen, sister, if you're still out there making sandwiches, answer me.

Daisy's Voice. Don't get impatient. I'll be there in a minute.

Spike. (*Crossing to desk.*) Well, she's still there. I guess you're too dumb to try any kind of game with me.

Ada. We wouldn't have to be very smart.

Glory. And you'd better not do any more of that shouting at Daisy either, unless you want Mother down here. She's a light sleeper and she's just waiting for something like this to happen

Spike. (*Slamming a desk drawer shut.*) Oh, Rats! This is the worst jam I ever got myself into. I sneak into a house and what do I find? Dames, dames, dames, hollering at me! I'm about ready to say you win, and walk out of here!

Ada. Walk out of here? What have we done?

Spike. Talk' Talk-talk-talk' The cops ought to use you for the third degree. I'm ready to walk out, I tell you

Glory. But you can't just walk out of here. Oh, no, not as easily as that.

Spike. Why not? I got feet ain't I?

Ada. Sure Big feet. But no brains.

Spike Listen . . .

Glory. You can't make a get-away as easily as you think You've made too many mistakes. You'll be lucky to get out of this with your *life!*

Spike. That's no lie Where I made my biggest mistake was coming to this screwy house in the first place. I'm willing to call everything quits. If there's anything I hate, it's a bunch of dumb, jabbering, senseless, empty-headed, dizzy, sleepy-eyed, skinny dames!

Ada.   We're not skinny, and you know it

Spike.   Sure, sure   But if you'll pardon me, I'll scram   It's ten to one there's nothing worth lifting in this house anyway

Ada.   Sour grapes

(MRS. BUSBY *enters from the stairs.   Her hair is in curlers, and she is wearing a rather over-elaborate night robe.   About fifty, only slightly gray, she doesn't look her age, but seems a match for her lively daughters.*)

Mrs. Busby.   How can anyone manage to sleep in this house! (*She sees* SPIKE)   Oh   how interesting'

Spike.   Holy cats'   Doesn't nobody sleep nights around here?

Glory.   Hello, Mom

Ada   Hello, Mom

Mrs. Busby.   Hello, girls   (*She smiles at* SPIKE *politely.*) I don't believe we've met   (*She crosses to* SPIKE.)   I'm Mrs. Busby   You're a burglar, I presume

Spike.   Yes, sure   and you're writing a mystery story!

Mrs Busby   You know about my story?

Glory.   We've been telling him, Mother   (*As* DAISY *comes in from the kitchen)*   Ah, food at last

(DAISY *is carrying a tray of sandwiches and coffee.   She sets it on the coffee table near the sofa, and the girls quickly help themselves)*

Daisy.   (*As she enters.*)   Here it is   Come and get it.   I couldn't find any mayonnaise

Spike.   So help me, I feel like a lamb among wolves!

Mrs. Busby.   (*Helpfully*)   Have a sandwich, Mister . . . er

Spike.   No, thanks

Daisy.   He's a burglar Mom   He won't eat.

Mrs. Busby. It's all so interesting. I'm writing a book. It's all about burglars, you know.

Spike. Yes, ma'am I know!

Mrs. Busby. The hero is a burglar named Orlando. You're name isn't Orlando, is it?

Spike. No, ma'am, it ain't.

Mrs. Busby. Well, what is it?

Spike. It's Spike

Mrs. Busby. Oh, of course. All burglars are nicknamed Spike. I mean your real name.

(*She sits in chair L.*)

Spike. Hell's fire! If you must know, my name is Hoginhurst. Clarence Hoginhurst.

(*He pulls the desk chair over to U.C., and sits.*)

Mrs. Busby. Oh, thank you, Mr. Hoginhurst.

Spike. Call me Spike.

Mrs. Busby. All right, Spike . . . Now, Mr. Hoginhurst, I'd like to tell you a bit about my book. (SPIKE *resigns himself.*) You see, my burglar, Orlando, has been out on a job, and his girl friend, named Cleotus, thinks he's been caught So she confesses to the crime. Now, of course, Orlando hasn't been caught, and he is faced with the problem of freedom, or whether he should give himself up for the sake of Cleotus You see, he's torn with passion between love and death, life and dishonor.

Spike. Yes'm

Mrs. Busby. Tell me, Mr Hoginhurst How should it end? Would you go to jail for Cleotus?

Spike. Why should I? I don't even know the dame.

Glory. Mom, you won't get anything out of him.

Ada. Just ask him simple questions. Ask him how **he gets** along.

Spike. (*Resentfully, shooting* ADA *a glance.*) I get along!

Mrs. Busby. Yes, I'm sure you do. But the first thing I'd like to know is, are you able to sleep nights?

Spike. No, ma'am. I work nights.

Mrs. Busby. I mean, do you spend sleepless hours because of your conscience? Doesn't it talk to you . . . torment you? Keep you awake?

Spike. No ma'am. Sometimes my wife does.

Mrs. Busby. Oh, heavens! You're very disappointing, Mr. Hoginhurst. You're very poor material Haven't you any vices?

Spike. Well, no I can't say I have. Except I rob a house now and then or snatch a handbag.

Mrs. Busby. I mean . . . like getting drunk. You do get drunk, don't you?

Spike. No, ma'am. It's bad for the system. Besides, it makes me sick.

Mrs. Busby. But surely you're addicted to something?

Spike. Does Coca Cola count?

Glory. I'm afraid you can't use him in your story, Mom, he's terrible.

Daisy. He doesn't even sound like a burglar to me.

Mrs. Busby. Detective books would be terribly dull if all burglars were like you, Mr Hoginhurst Don't you ever do anything desperate?

Spike. Well .   I don't know

    (*He scratches his head with the point of his gun. It alarms him when he sees what he's doing.*)

No . . . I don't think so.

Glory. (*Crossing to the food.*) Let's wait till we get another one, Mom

Mrs. Busby. Now, Glory, don't be rude. (*To* SPIKE.) I'd

like to find out something about your methods, Mr Hoginhurst.
Take this case, for instance Did you study our house and the
habits of our family before you undertook this job?

Spike.   Study the habits of this family? No, ma'am

Mrs. Busby.   (*Crossing to* SPIKE) You mean you didn't
even know who lived here?

Spike.   If I did I wouldn'ta come!

Mrs. Busby.   You mean to say that you risked coming into
this house without knowing when we went to bed, when we got
up, or when we came home nights?

Spike.   I didn't know nothing

Ada.   He's a dodo, Mom   He's pulled worse boners than that
He even left footprints on your new grass

Spike.   Oh, let up about that front lawn, will you?

Mrs. Busby.   Well, supposing you were caught tomorrow,
what would you give for an alibi?

Spike.   Alibi?

Mrs. Busby.   Certainly If they accused you of being here,
you'd have to prove you were somewhere else

Spike.   Well   I could say I went to a movie

   (*A loud groan from everyone shows* SPIKE *this wasn't the
   right answer.*)

Mrs. Busby.   A movie! Do you mean to say that's all the
alibi you've established   that you went to a movie?

Spike.   (*Crossing wearily D.L , then turns to* MRS BUSBY)
Listen, lady, all I wanted to do was drop in and pick up a little
pocket money   I don't want to write a detective book.

Mrs. Busby.   You just wanted to drop in and pick up a little
pocket money!

Glory.   (*Suddenly.*) Mom, I don't trust him!

Ada.   He sounds like a phony to me

Daisy.   I'll bet anything he's a fake

Mrs. Busby.   Well .   Mr. Hoginhurst?

Spike   Well . . . I . . . the truth is

   (*He crosses C. nervously, stalling for words.*)

Mrs. Busby.   The truth is you're a fraud and a cheat. Passing yourself off on honest folk as a professional burglar   You're a lying, underhanded   counterfeit.   (*With feeling.*)   You ought to be ashamed.

Daisy.   He's no good.   Why don't you call the cops?

Ada.   Oh, don't bother.   The cops will catch him soon enough   Let him go home.

   (*She crosses to sofa, eating.*)

Daisy.   I got a good look at his gun . .   and you know what's more?   I don't think it's even loaded.

Glory.   Not even loaded?

Spike.   Well . . . you see . . . you see . . .

   (SPIKE *is unable to answer; becomes embarrassed.*)

Mrs. Busby.   Bless me!   I believe my daughter's right!   Mr. Hoginhurst, I view you with intense suspicion.   I think we're entitled to some explanation.

Spike.   (*Whiningly.*)   Why don't you let me alone!   This is a free country ain't it?   (MRS. BUSBY *crosses to R.C. to usher the girls out.* SPIKE *goes U.C. He moves a chair and sits in it.*)

Mrs. Busby.   You girls run along to bed.   I want to talk to this presumtuous Clarence Hoginhurst alone.   And, Daisy . . take the tray back to the kitchen.

Daisy.   Okay, Mom.   Go easy with him.

   (DAISY *takes tray and exits R.*)

Glory.   (*As she and* ADA *start L.*)   Good night, Mom.   Don't be too rough on him.

Ada.   Good night, Mom.   Come up early.

Mrs. Busby. Good night, dears.

(GLORY *and* ADA *exit to stairs.* MRS. BUSBY *follows them
L., then turns back.*)

Well?

Spike. (*Sheepishly.*) Well what?

Mrs. Busby. (*Crossing to* SPIKE.) You ought to be thoroughly ashamed of yourself. You're a perfect flop as a burglar. I don't know who you are, but you're a disgrace to the profession.

Spike. (*Going to coffee table; sitting on sofa, miserably*) Oh, I know, I know I'm a total failure I try terribly hard, really I do . . but . well, I always make a complete mess of it If people hadn't been so kind and considerate, I'd have ended up long ago. (*He suddenly blurts this out*) I'm even afraid to carry a loaded gun! If the darn' thing went off, I'd faint

Mrs. Busby. It's too bad For a burglar, you look as if you might have lots of talent.

(*She goes over to* SPIKE; *pats his shoulder helpfully.*)

Spike. Listen, please promise me one thing Just don't tell anybody. Don't let it get around what a flop I am Gosh, I haven't been able to pull a decent job in years!

Mrs. Busby. In years?

Spike. That's the truth It's the administration (*With a sigh*) What time is it?

Mrs. Busby. It's after one

Spike. Gosh, it's getting late Do you mind if I call my wife?

Mrs. Busby. No, I guess not
(*She indicates the phone on the desk.*)

Spike. Thanks
(*He goes to the telephone, dials a number, waits.*)

Spike. (*While waiting for an answer.*) I'm supposed to get some things at the store. (*Into phone*) Oh . hello, dear,

is that you? . . . This is Clarence. . . . Yes, dear. I'm . . . I'm . . . well, right now I'm opening a safe. (*He gives* MRS. BUSBY *a sheepish look.*) . . Yes, dear . . . Well, I'll be home a little late Probably won't get home till after six . . Yes, dear Now, what was it you wanted at the store? Eggs? . . Yes, dear Eggs . . . a pound of butter . . loaf of bread. . . . Yes, dear, I will . . . Yes, dear . Good night.
    (*He hangs up.*)
Do you think I'll find a delicatessen open some place?

    Mrs. Busby. Do you *buy* your butter and eggs?

    Spike. Well, yes, it's safer

    Mrs. Busby. Tell me, Mr. Hoginhurst, since you're such a flop as a burglar, how do you manage to make a living?

    Spike. Well, my wife thinks I steal everything

    Mrs. Busby. Well, yes; but you have to have money to buy butter and eggs

    Spike. I hate to tell you. Promise you'll keep it secret.

    Mrs. Busby. Yes, I promise.

    Spike. You wouldn't tell my wife?

    Mrs. Busby. No, I won't tell. What do you do?

    Spike. I got a early morning paper route.

    Mrs. Busby. Paper route?

    Spike. (*Sadly*) Yes. (*He sighs.*) I'd better get at it too, if I want to get home It takes about three hours You wouldn't want to subscribe to the *Morning News* would you?

    Mrs. Busby. Not tonight

    Spike. I'd better be on my way now You won't tell?

    Mrs. Busby. No, certainly not. But don't go across that newly seeded terrace again Go out the front way.

    Spike. Yes, ma'am.
    (*He goes to archway U.L.*)

Mrs. Busby. And if you can't find a store open, come back and I'll lend you some eggs

Spike. Yes, ma'am. Gee, thanks. Good night.

Mrs. Busby. Good night.

  (SPIKE *goes out.* DAISY *enters from R.*)

Daisy. I put everything away, but I stacked the dishes. Has he gone?

Mrs. Busby. Yes. But he may be back after some eggs. Do we have plenty?

Daisy. I think so Anyway Pop is bringing some home. Didn't you put them on his list?

Mrs. Busby. That's so, I did. Incidentally, it's getting late. It's time your father was *here.*

Daisy. It's early yet. What house is Pop robbing tonight, Mom?

Mrs. Busby. The Beardsly's, on the west side. It's only about seven blocks away I don't see why your father said he wouldn't be home before six in the morning! (*She pauses for a moment.*) Say, I wonder if *he* . . . Humpf! Come to bed, Daisy. I think I'll have a talk with your father when he comes home!

CURTAIN

Also By
Guernsey Le Pelley

Absolutely Murder

Please visit our website **bakersplays.com** for complete
descriptions and licensing information